Cory Coleman, Grade 2

Larry Dane Brimner

Cory Coleman, Grade 2

Illustrated by Karen Ritz

A Redfeather Chapter Book

Henry Holt and Company • New York

Published by Henry Holt and Company, Inc.,
115 West 18th Street, New York, New York 10011.
Published in Canada by Fitzhenry & Whiteside Limited.
195 Allstate Parkway, Markham, Ontario L3R 4T8.

Library of Congress Cataloging-in-Publication Data
Brimner, Larry Dane.
    Cory Coleman, grade 2 / by Larry Dane Brimner : illustrated by
Karen Ritz.
        (A Redfeather book)
        Summary: Seven-year-old Cory Coleman's birthday party is ruined by
the class bully, who turns out not to be such a bully in the end.
        [1. Bullies—Fiction.   2. Friendship—Fiction.   3. Schools—
Fiction.]   I. Ritz, Karen, ill.   II. Title.   III. Title: Cory
Coleman, grade two.   IV. Series.
PZ7.B767Cn   1990
[E]—dc20   89-24694

ISBN 0-8050-1312-1 (hardcover)
10 9 8 7 6 5 4 3 2
ISBN 0-8050-1844-1 (paperback)
10 9 8 7

Henry Holt books are available at special discounts
for bulk purchases for sales promotions, premiums,
fund-raising, or educational use. Special editions
or book excerpts can also be created to specification.

First published in hardcover in 1990 by
Henry Holt and Company, Inc.
First Redfeather paperback edition, 1991

Printed in Mexico.

For John Kendryna, Jr.,
who was never a bully
—L.D.B.

Contents

Cory Coleman, Grade 2

1 · Waiting

"**H**ey, watch it!" Cory Coleman snapped. He jerked back his hands.

Delphinius Lane chuckled. The book had barely missed Cory's fingers.

"I suppose you're going to make me," Delphinius challenged.

"Well—" Cory hesitated. He bit his thumbnail while he thought. There was no way he was going to *make* Delphinius do anything. Delphinius was the biggest kid in class.

"Delphinius," said Ms. Ricks. She sighed. "Reading can't begin until everyone has a book. I know you are going to be an outstanding book monitor this week."

"Yes, Ms. Ricks," Delphinius said, as polite as could be. Then he smirked at Cory. His hand made a slicing motion at his neck. He whispered, "Next time, Curly, I'll get your whole hand."

Delphinius continued down the row of desks. He dropped a book on each one.

Cory pulled at a snip of yellow hair. When he let go, it sprang back into place—*boing*—right over his right eye.

"Worms," Cory said. He said that when he was cross. "Worms to you, Dumb-phinius!" But he didn't say it so loud that Delphinius could hear.

Dumb-phinius. Cory had thought of it first. Back in September.

Delphinius was supposed to be in third grade. But he had been held back. When Cory found out about that, he got the idea. *Dumb*-phinius. Cory thought it fit better than *Del*phinius.

And it stuck. Everyone began to call him Dumb-phinius—as long as Delphinius wasn't around to hear.

Ms. Ricks said, "Open your books to page twelve. After we have read the story, we will answer some questions. Pay very close attention."

"Can I read?" asked C.J. Lewis. She waved one hand round and round like the propeller of a helicop-

ter. The other hand fished inside her briefcase for her glasses.

"Thank you, Constance," said Ms. Ricks. "You *may*."

"C.J.," corrected C.J., and she began to read.

Cory pretended to pay very close attention. But he was not thinking about reading. He was thinking about show-and-tell. Today, Cory had something to tell. He sneaked a peek at the clock.

The big black hand was only on the two. It had to go all the way to the nine before it would be time for show-and-tell. The minute hand just poked along— *tock tock tock*—in no more hurry than a snail in cool shade.

Cory sighed. "Worms!" he said. The word just slipped out.

"Cory," said Ms. Ricks, "will you read next?" Ms. Ricks did not like it when people let words slip.

Cory read. He was a good reader. He liked to read. In fact, Cory liked everything about school. Except maybe arithmetic. But even that seemed to be getting easier now that everyone in Ms. Ricks's class had an arithmetic buddy.

Cory finished the paragraph.

"Delphinius, please read next," said Ms. Ricks.

Delphinius looked up, surprised. He'd been poking around inside his desk. And his book wasn't even open.

Ms. Ricks did not like it when people did not pay attention, either.

Delphinius turned red. He was not a good reader. He opened his book. He tried to look at Elizabeth Ann Martin's book to find out the page. She covered the page with her arm.

Josh Reynolds held up his book for Delphinius to see. He pointed at the word Delphinius was to read.

Ms. Ricks waited for Delphinius to find the place. "Delphinius, please read next," she said again.

Delphinius read. " 'Th— the dr— dream— er—' "

" 'Drummer,' " whispered Elizabeth Ann.

"I know," said Delphinius.

"Then why didn't you *say* it?" asked Elizabeth Ann. "Ms. Ricks, we don't have time for *him* to read. Let someone else read."

Cory looked at the clock. There was *not* time for Delphinius to read. The big hand was on the nine.

Ms. Ricks looked at Elizabeth Ann. She used her one-eyebrow-up look. Everyone knew what that meant.

"Elizabeth Ann," said Ms. Ricks. "I am certain you did not mean that the way it sounded. I know you want everyone to have a turn to read."

Elizabeth Ann swallowed hard. Then she mumbled something that sounded like an apology.

"Delphinius," said Ms. Ricks. "Would you like to continue, please?"

Delphinius banged his book shut. He folded his arms and scrunched his mouth into a tight little circle. When he did, the freckles on his face smashed into each other and became one big freckle.

Cory thought, Delphinius looks like a spot of rust. A giant spot of rust that isn't going to read no matter what.

Ms. Ricks sounded tired when she said, "Tim, will you finish reading for Delphinius, please?"

Tim Giovanni finished the story. He was in Cory's reading group. He was a good reader too.

"Please take out a piece of paper and copy the questions off the chalkboard," said Ms. Ricks. "You may answer them for homework."

Everyone moaned when she said "homework."

"We could answer them now," she said, "but then there would be no time for show-and-tell."

"We should do it now," said Amy Andrews. "We need to play after school."

"After school," said C.J., "I have a Future Leaders meeting." She snapped her briefcase shut as though that settled it.

"No," said Josh. "I brought something for show-and-tell."

"And I have something too," said Cory.

"Let's vote," said Ms. Ricks.

2 · Show-and-tell

"Show-and-tell wins," said Ms. Ricks. "Copy the questions. And don't forget the heading."

The big black minute hand wasn't a snail anymore. Now it seemed to race—*tickety tock, tickety tock*—toward the twelve. Cory hurried to print the heading onto his paper. He wrote: *Cory Coleman, Grade 2, Reading.*

Worms! Cory thought. Wasted words. Wasted time.

In no time at all, Josh raised his hand. "I'm done," he announced. "Can I share first?"

"I should be first," said Elizabeth Ann. "I'm a girl, and girls always go first." She pointed her nose in the air.

Cory copied the last question. He folded the paper inside his book. Then everyone seemed to finish.

"Let's not squabble," Ms. Ricks said. "We'll do what is fair. We'll draw straws."

"Oh, let her go first," said Josh. "We don't have time for straws. She's probably got something dumb to share anyway."

"It is not dumb," Elizabeth Ann said. Then she told all about being in her aunt's wedding.

The minute hand was getting closer and closer to the twelve. Cory thought, Elizabeth Ann's show-and-tell *is* dumb, and if she doesn't hurry up, I won't have time to tell my news.

"And— *and*," said Elizabeth Ann, "I caught the bouquet!"

Finally, Cory thought. Then he whispered, "Hurry up, Josh. There isn't much time."

"We're waiting, Josh," said Ms. Ricks.

Josh dug around in his desk. Then he buried his head in his book bag.

"Just a minute," Josh said. He ran to the coat room and rummaged through his coat pockets.

The minute hand was almost on the twelve.

When Josh turned around, he said, "I— I guess I forgot it."

Cory thought, Worms! Worms! Worms! That is just like Josh Reynolds. He can't remember from one second to the next.

"Cory," said Ms. Ricks. "What did you want to share?"

Cory sat up straight and tall. "It's something important," he said. "It's really great."

Everyone was watching Cory. The clock's big black hand skipped a minute closer to the twelve.

"Saturday's my birthday, and I'll be seven," said Cory.

"It's about time, Curly," said Delphinius. He smirked. Everyone else oohed and aahed.

Cory tried to pretend that Delphinius wasn't there. "I— I'm having a party. A skating party. And everyone is invited."

Everyone oohed and aahed even louder. Except Delphinius. Then the clock's big black hand skipped to the twelve, and the bell rang.

"A skating party will be fun," said Ms. Ricks. "Right now, though, I have yard duty. We'll talk about the party tomorrow. Push in your chairs. Everyone may leave."

Suddenly there was the clatter of chairs and the buzz of voices and the shuffle of feet.

"Don't forget to do your homework," reminded Ms. Ricks.

Cory watched Delphinius push and shove his way toward the door. A book slammed to the floor. It belonged to Delphinius. Delphinius turned and kicked the book. It skidded between the legs of the desks.

"Delphinius!" Ms. Ricks said. "I'd like to see you."

Delphinius jerked to a stop. He jabbed his fists into his pockets. He lowered his head. He shuffled to Ms. Ricks's desk.

Cory picked up the book and put it on top of Delphinius's desk.

"Thank you, Cory," said Ms. Ricks.

Cory slipped out of the room. But instead of leaving, like he knew he should, he stood in the hall just outside the doorway. If Delphinius got a scolding, Cory wanted to know all about it.

But Cory was disappointed. Instead of scolding

him, Ms. Ricks told Delphinius how important she thought he was because he was the oldest and could set an example.

"I'm counting on you," Ms. Ricks said to Delphinius.

Cory couldn't believe his ears. He thought, If it was anyone else—

At that moment Delphinius darted out of the doorway. He rounded the corner so suddenly that Cory didn't see him coming. Delphinius must not have seen Cory either. *Smack!* Delphinius smashed right into Cory.

Cory thought, "Uh-oh."

But Delphinius just gave him a mean look. Then he hurried out of the building.

Jingle. Jangle.

Cory heard keys. It was Ms. Ricks rushing out of the room. She was surprised to see Cory.

"Cory," she said, locking the door. "I thought you'd be on your way home by now."

"I'm waiting for my friend," Cory said. He nodded toward the closed door across the hall.

"Your birthday certainly sounds exciting. Am I invited to your party?"

"Sure," said Cory.

Ms. Ricks smiled and headed toward the playground.

At the same time, Cory was wishing Delphinius would find something better to do than go to his party.

3 · The Delphinius Problem

Cory waited in the hall.

For a while he counted squares of tile on the floor. Just the dirty brown ones, not the yellow ones. Then a voice interrupted him.

"Ms. Ricks *never* makes you guys line up." It was Baltimore Romero. He ran up to Cory.

Baltimore and Cory had been best friends ever since preschool. Even before. They had always lived next door to each other, and they had done everything together until this year.

This year Baltimore was in the other second grade, with Mrs. Culbertson. Mrs. Culbertson was old, *old*, OLD. And she was mean. She made her class line up for everything. They lined up to go outside. To come inside. To sharpen pencils. To pass papers. Some older kids said she made kids line up to be sick. They also said she was a witch. Cory was glad he was in Ms. Ricks's room.

"You *always* get out early," Baltimore said. The pair walked out the door, down the steps, and past a coffee-colored statue of Ulysses S. Grant. Mr. Grant had been the eighteenth president of the United States. It said so on the block of shiny gray stone under the statue. Under that, on a bigger block of the same kind of stone, it said:

GRANT SCHOOL

FOUNDED 1967

Cory saluted as he went by the statue. Then he teased, "You always get out late."

Baltimore made cross-eyes at Cory. "It's Mrs. Culbertson's fault," he said. "It's all that lining up she makes us do. It's just not fair."

Cory looked around. "What's not fair is Dumbphinius Lane," he said. He was serious now.

"Argf!" Baltimore said. Delphinius had given Baltimore a bloody nose on the first day of school—just because Baltimore had told him third grade was upstairs. "I hope *he's* not coming to your party."

"My mom said to invite everyone or no one," Cory said.

"What's that mean?" asked Baltimore.

"It means Dumb-phinius is coming," Cory said. "Unless he has something better to do."

"What's better than skating?" Baltimore asked. Then he added, "You'll be sorry if he comes."

Cory knew Baltimore was right. Delphinius bullied everybody. Especially Cory. It had been that way since September. And although he wasn't very good at arithmetic, there was one thing Cory knew for sure: Dumb-phinius + party = *trouble.*

Something had to be done. But what?

The pair crossed Maple Leaf Avenue and turned down Orchard Lane. Baltimore had an idea.

He said, "Don't tell Dumb-phinius where your skating party will be."

"That wouldn't work," Cory said. "Everyone knows there's only one rink in Northwood."

"So tell him we're skating at the pond." Baltimore seemed to think about that. "No good," he said. "It's only November. The pond isn't frozen yet."

"Worms!" Cory said. "It's no use."

Cory turned up his walk. Baltimore tagged along

behind him. When they reached the porch, Cory un-
zipped his jacket and fished inside his shirt for the
key that hung on a chain around his neck.

"Presto!" he said, and held up the key. He un-
locked the back door.

Both boys banged their books down on the kitchen
table. Cory dragged a chair over to the sink. He
pushed a flashlight out of the way and stood on top
of the counter. While he reached up for two glasses,
Baltimore took a carton of milk out of the refrigera-
tor.

When they sat down at the table, Baltimore
scrunched his eyebrows together. That made him
look like a fuzzy black caterpillar was resting right
in the middle of his forehead. "What did you just
say?" he asked.

"Nothing," Cory said, and lifted the top off of the
cookie jar.

"No. Just now. Outside. You said something," Baltimore said. He helped himself to a cookie.
"Mmmm," he added. "Chocolate chip."

Cory chewed on his thumbnail and thought. At the
same time, he held up a cookie with his other hand.
He studied the cookie as though it might help him

to remember what he'd just said. He shrugged his shoulders. "Only thing I can remember," he said, and popped the cookie into his mouth, "isspwesdo."

"Huh?"

Cory gulped. "Presto," he repeated.

"That's it!" said Baltimore. "That's it."

"What's it?" Sometimes Cory thought Baltimore was a little strange.

"*Presto.*" Baltimore snapped his fingers together. "No more Dumb-phinius Lane."

Cory was really confused now.

Baltimore sighed. "It's your birthday. Ask your mom for that magic kit down at Carson's Toys and make him disappear. I bet it tells how to do it."

This time Cory sighed. It was the dumbest idea. It would never work. Magicians didn't really make people disappear. Besides, if somehow it did work, he figured he'd get into trouble. A lot of trouble.

It would be a neat trick, though. Cory made his fingers snap. He smiled as he thought about Delphinius disappearing into a puff of smoke.

Cory bit at a sliver of thumbnail, and carefully pulled it loose with his teeth. "If it didn't work," he said, "Dumb-phinius would kill me. If it did, my mom would take care of the job for him. Anyway, I already told her I want a Monster Wheels with power remote." He flicked the tiny piece of thumbnail toward the floor.

"Yeah?" said Baltimore. He seemed to forget the Delphinius problem. "Do you think you'll really get one?"

Cory shifted his shoulders. "Mom's sold a lot of houses. She said it's been a good year, so maybe. But—maybe not. You never know until you open your presents."

Baltimore made cross-eyes at Cory. When he did, his black eyes sparkled with mystery. "What do you mean, you never know until you open your presents? Don't you ever peek?"

Cory shook his head. The mop of yellow curls danced.

"Never?"

Cory shook his head again.

"Well, I always know what I'm getting," said Baltimore. "Mom and Dad hide everything in the basement. Right behind the furnace. All it takes is a peek. I— I like to know what I'm getting. Then I can practice being surprised."

"Practice?" Cory didn't understand why someone would need to practice being surprised. Either you were or you weren't. What did practice have to do with it?

"All right," said Baltimore, "so I just can't stand it when someone knows something I don't."

"I like to be surprised," Cory said.

"But all it takes is a peek," Baltimore said again. "Let's look."

"I— I don't know," said Cory. "It's— it's sneaky." But Cory *was* curious. He had wanted a Monster Wheels for a long time.

"Come on," said Baltimore. "What's wrong with a little peek?"

A peek. Just a little peek, Cory thought.

Then Cory repeated Baltimore's words. "What's wrong with a little peek?"

4 · Monster Wheels

It didn't take long to find it. Cory lifted a box of his mother's old shoes out of the way. Behind that, right on the top shelf in her closet, sat another box. A smaller box.

On the front of the smaller box was a picture. It showed a truck with giant wheels, monster wheels. It was driving over other, ordinary trucks. Smashing them. Crunching them like toys.

The picture was all Cory needed to see. He yipped with joy. "A Monster Wheels! I'm really getting a Monster Wheels." He let his fingers gently touch the picture.

"Let me see." Baltimore climbed on top of the chair and pushed beside Cory. For a moment both boys stared at the picture.

"Let's try it out." It was Baltimore.

"I don't know," said Cory. "It's not right."

"It's *your* birthday present, isn't it?" Baltimore said.

"Yeah, but—" Cory thought. He bit at his thumb-nail. There wasn't enough left to catch between his teeth. He bit off a pinch of skin instead. "S— something might happen."

"Like what?" asked Baltimore. He crossed, then uncrossed his eyes. "It's a Monster Wheels. A Monster Wheels is indestructible. It says so on TV."

"If my mom ever found out, she'd kill me," Cory said.

"She'll never know."

Cory scrunched up his face. "It's not a good idea." This time his voice was weak.

"Come on," said Baltimore. "We'll stack up some shoes and see if it climbs over them. Then we'll put it back just like we found it."

Cory sighed. Then he whispered, "I guess it'll be okay. But Mom will be home from work soon."

"All right!" Baltimore slapped his knee and jumped from the chair with the box in his hands. He sat on the floor and took out the truck. It was hot red. With giant black wheels. Monster wheels.

Cory stacked up some of his mother's shoes.

Baltimore aimed the remote control at the truck. He pushed on the lever. Nothing happened.

"Something's wrong," Baltimore said. He shook the control. He banged it against the floor. Then he took aim again.

Still nothing happened.

Cory felt his heart hop into his throat and stomach at the same time. "You broke it," he whispered.

Baltimore didn't seem to hear. He wiggled a clip and the end of the control box popped open.

Cory's eyes became as big as the truck's monster wheels. He gasped and clamped a hand over his mouth to keep his heart from flying out of his body.

"Needs batteries," Baltimore said.

Cory didn't move. His hand was still pressed against his mouth.

"Cor, it needs batteries," Baltimore repeated. He held up the control box and showed Cory where two batteries should be.

Slowly, Cory let out his breath. "Batteries?" he said, like he didn't know what batteries were.

"You know. To make it go."

Cory's funny feeling was gone as quickly as it had come. His heart went back to where it should be.

Cory remembered the flashlight on top of the kitchen counter. There were batteries inside the flashlight. "Just a minute," he said, and disappeared from his mother's bedroom.

When he returned, Cory tossed the flashlight to Baltimore. Baltimore took out the batteries and slid them into the control box.

He aimed the control at the Monster Wheels. He pushed the lever forward.

Nothing happened.

Baltimore jiggled the lever back and forth, side to side. Nothing happened again.

"Maybe the batteries are upside down," Cory said.

Baltimore turned the batteries around and jiggled the lever one more time.

It didn't move. The shiny red machine that was supposed to tackle mountains and trample over other trucks didn't move.

Cory's funny feeling returned. "I knew it," he said. "I just knew it. All that shaking and banging. And now it doesn't work."

"Quick!," said Baltimore. "Let's put it away. Like we found it."

"Worms! Why did I listen to you?" Cory asked, jamming his thumb into his mouth. He caught another piece of skin between his teeth and pulled it off. A tiny bead of blood formed where the skin had been.

Baltimore was already packing the Monster Wheels back into its box. He slid the box back onto the shelf. "She'll never know it's broken," he said.

"Until my birthday," said Cory. He licked the blood off his thumb, then twisted the cap back onto the flashlight. Now he wished his birthday would never come.

5 · Saturday

Tuesday.
Wednesday.
Thursday.
Friday.
The days whizzed by, and suddenly it was Saturday morning.

Cory opened his eyes. Sunlight spilled through the bedroom window. He lay in bed and tried hard not to think about Delphinius or about the Monster Wheels. But the harder he tried not to think about them, the more he worried.

Probably Delphinius would make trouble.

Probably his mother would be angry when she found out that the Monster Wheels was broken.

Probably?

Cory shook his head. No. No probably about it. Delphinius would make trouble. His mother would be angry.

Cory pulled the covers over his head. He clamped both eyes shut tight. "Go back to sleep. Go back to sleep," he told himself again and again. But it was no use.

"Rise and shine." It was Cory's mother.

Cory groaned. He poked his head from beneath the covers.

"It's time for the birthday boy to get up," Cory's mother said. "Baltimore will be here soon. It wouldn't be polite for us to be late."

Cory looked at his mother. He smiled weakly. Late sounded good. Maybe he could even miss this birthday.

His mother, arms crossed, waited at the door for him to stir. It was clear she would have nothing to do with missed birthdays. She stood there until both of his feet were on the floor and in motion toward the bathroom.

Later, Cory dragged himself into the kitchen. Spicy smells greeted him. Cinnamon smells. Vanilla smells. Banana smells.

It was his favorite breakfast. French toast. With sliced bananas on top.

But Cory wasn't hungry. He swirled the French toast around on his plate.

"Don't you feel well?" his mother asked. She felt his forehead. "I thought you liked French toast."

Cory didn't feel well at all. But he wasn't sick.

He wanted to tell his mother all about the broken Monster Wheels. Something stopped him.

"I— I'm okay," he said instead, and forced a piece of French toast into his mouth.

"Well, have I got a surprise for you," his mother said. She set a package on the table. Balloons floated across the package. Red balloons. Yellow balloons. Green balloons. The package was much too large for a Monster Wheels.

But Cory knew his mother's tricks. Inside the big package would be a smaller package. And maybe another and another. But finally there would be the Monster Wheels. The broken Monster Wheels. Cory was certain of that.

"Do you want to open your present now?" his mother asked. "Or after the skating party?"

There was a knock at the door. Cory jumped to answer it.

"Happy birthday!" It was Baltimore. Cory was glad for that. He didn't want to open his mother's present to him.

Baltimore handed Cory a card in one hand and a present in the other. "It's bubble gum," Baltimore said. "Fifteen flavors."

"That's great," said Cory. "Thanks."

Cory thought about opening Baltimore's present to him. They could share the gum. But if he opened one present, he would have to open the other. The present from his mother. He opened the card instead and passed it to his mother to read.

His mother finished reading the card. She glanced at the clock over the kitchen door.

"Look at the time!" she said. "We'd better run."

Cory grabbed his coat off the hook by the door and did just that.

6 · The Ice House

"Worms!" Cory said. He nudged Baltimore in the ribs with his elbow and pointed.

There was Delphinius. He stood in the doorway under a sign that said THE ICE HOUSE. He had a pair of black skates hanging over his shoulder.

Cory's mother wheeled the red Subaru into a parking space. She got out of the front seat. Baltimore got out of the back. Cory sank between the two seats. Maybe he could hide out until it was all over.

"Cory, what has gotten into you?" said Cory's mother.

There would be no hiding out. Cory knew that from the tone of his mother's voice—an I've-had-enough-of-this tone. He eased out of the backseat. He trailed his mother and Baltimore toward The Ice House.

''Pop works Saturdays,'' said Delphinius. He shifted the skates. Hockey skates. The silver blades flashed in the morning sunlight. ''He had to drop me off early.''

Cory introduced Delphinius.

''I hope you haven't been waiting too long,'' said Cory's mother.

''No, ma'am,'' said Delphinius. ''Only about half an hour.'' Delphinius flashed his sweet-as-can-be smile.

''Everything's been taken care of, so you boys go on inside,'' suggested Cory's mother. ''Cory and I should wait for the others.''

Delphinius pushed through the door.

Baltimore dillydallied, shifting from one foot to the other. ''Thanks, Mrs. C., but— but I'll wait with Cor.''

''Don't be silly,'' Cory's mother said. ''We only have the rink for two hours.'' She inched Baltimore through the door. ''Besides, Cory needs somebody to keep Delphinius company until the others come.''

The glass doors swung closed, leaving Cory and his mother on the outside and Baltimore on the inside. Baltimore looked like a scared puppy.

"Nice boy," Cory's mother said.

Cory didn't say anything. But he thought, Nice boy—for a bully.

Just then Amy Andrews raced up on her bicycle. She screeched to a stop and jumped off. "I'm ready!" she said. "Where's the ice?"

She was through the door before Cory could tell her.

Elizabeth Ann Martin and Tim Giovanni rattled up in Elizabeth Ann's mother's car. Elizabeth Ann and Tim lived next door to each other.

"Happy birthday, Cory," Tim said.

Then Elizabeth Ann's mother's car backfired. It belched smoke. Elizabeth Ann turned red. She looked like she wanted to disappear.

"You can get some skates inside," Cory said.

Elizabeth Ann dashed through the doors. Tim followed her.

Ms. Ricks came next. She had on pants. Cory had never seen her in pants before. She always wore a dress to school.

Pants are smart, thought Cory. No pizza knees, with pants.

A long, black Mercedes pulled up next. C.J. Lewis

swung open the door and got out. She dragged a white leather bag with her. She must have read Cory's thoughts.

"My skates," C.J. said. She glanced at her watch. "I thought you said this party began at nine."

"It is nine," Cory said.

"It is exactly three minutes before nine," C.J. corrected.

"Well—" Cory said.

"Will it be over with at eleven?" C.J. asked. "Or *around* eleven? I need to know, so Father will know when to come get me."

Cory shrugged. "It will be over with at eleven." Then he heard C.J tell her father to pick her up at around eleven.

Eleven. Around eleven. It's the same thing, Cory thought.

Before long everybody was there except Josh Reynolds.

"Are you sure he said he could come?" asked Cory's mother.

Cory nodded. Then he thought about Josh. Josh, who wore the same pants to school everyday. Josh, whose father left one day and didn't come back.

Cory felt sad and lucky at the same time.

"He probably decided not to come," Cory said. He started to go inside.

"Hey, Cory!"

It was Josh. He was waving, and tearing across the parking lot. He had on his school pants.

"Happy— birth— day," he gasped, between gulps of air.

Cory went inside with Josh. For a minute he forgot about the broken Monster Wheels. He forgot about Delphinius Lane.

Everyone else who needed skates had gotten them from the bearded man behind the skate counter. They were already on the ice.

Josh and Cory went to the counter and picked out their sizes. They went to a bench to put on their skates.

Baltimore glided up to them and stopped. "Hurry up, you guys," he said. "This is great."

And then, just when Cory decided it felt good to be seven, he heard something he had heard before.

"It's about time, Curly."

7 · Guilty, as Charged

Cory gulped. His mouth dropped open.

Baltimore pushed away from Delphinius. Out of striking distance.

"I've already paid you back," Delphinius said to Baltimore. To Cory he said, "But now it's your turn." He grinned. Then he wobbled away.

"What did he mean by that?" asked Josh.

Cory pressed his thumb between his teeth. He bit off a sliver of skin. He seemed to study the small, red bubble of blood that formed.

Cory sucked the blood from his thumb. Trouble, he thought. Delphinius means trouble.

Across the ice, Delphinius smacked into Amy. *Crash!*

Amy skidded to the ice on her knees. "Watch out, Delphinius!" she cried.

Crash! Delphinius bumped into Elizabeth Ann.

Elizabeth Ann banged into the wall and bounced into Tim. Tim belly-flopped onto the ice.

"Delphinius!" they both hollered at once.

"You better do something," Josh said to Cory.

"There he goes again," said Baltimore. Delphinius smashed into C.J. and sent her flying across the ice on her rump.

"What can I do?" Cory asked.

Josh and Baltimore shifted their shoulders. "You better think of something," Baltimore said. "If you don't, he's going to kill somebody."

"Why me?" Cory asked. He felt awful. This was the worst birthday he could remember.

"It's your party," Baltimore answered. "I told you you'd be sorry if Dumb-phinius came."

Cory didn't need to be reminded. He tried not to be angry. He knew how Baltimore felt about Delphinius. Then he remembered that Baltimore also told him that the Monster Wheels was indestructible.

Suddenly, Cory *was* angry. "Worms!" he shouted. He hopped to his feet and jumped onto the ice.

Cory glided swiftly and smoothly over the ice. He passed Amy and Elizabeth Ann and Tim and C.J.

and the others. Finally he caught up with Delphinius. By then Delphinius was near Ms. Ricks and Cory's mother.

Delphinius held out his arms like a tightrope walker. He wobbled this way and that.

Cory skimmed the ice beside Delphinius. "You have to stop crashing into people," Cory hollered. "You're going to hurt somebody."

Now they were closer to Ms. Ricks and Cory's mother.

Delphinius pretended not to hear. "What?" he hollered back to Cory. Wobble. Wobble.

"Be careful!" Cory yelled. "You're not being funny."

By then, they were next to Ms. Ricks and Cory's mother. Delphinius stopped wobbling. He turned sharply. His blades flashed. Suddenly, Delphinius skidded right in front of Ms. Ricks and Cory's mother.

Ms. Ricks tumbled to the ice. She reached out to Cory's mother.

Cory's mother lost her balance. She toppled on top of Ms. Ricks.

Cory froze. There were so many people tumbling

and skidding and spinning, he didn't know what to do.

When everyone stopped skidding, there was a heap of people on the ice. Cory's mother. Ms. Ricks. Delphinius.

"Delphinius, are you all right?" asked Cory's mother and Ms. Ricks at the same time.

Delphinius nodded his head.

Cory's mother looked at Ms. Ricks.

"Just a bit shaken," said Ms. Ricks.

"Me too," said Cory's mother.

Then Delphinius broke into tears. "Why did you push me?" he cried. He was looking right at Cory. "We might have got hurt."

Cory was too surprised to say he hadn't pushed anyone. He was too surprised to say anything at all.

The three untangled and brushed themselves off. Stiffly Cory's mother skated toward him.

Cory's mother didn't ask if it had been an accident. She didn't ask if Delphinius was telling the truth. She only said, "Apologize." When she said it, just her lips moved. Her teeth were sealed tight.

Cory was too stunned to do anything else. "I— I'm s— sorry," he stammered.

Then his mother latched onto his arm and skated toward the benches. It was all Cory could do to keep up with her.

When she reached the edge of the ice, she pointed at a bench. "I think you need some time to think," she said. Then she skated away.

Cory plopped down on the bench. No trial. No jury. Just guilty, as charged.

Across the ice, Delphinius whirled. First on one leg. Then on the other. Round. Round. Round.

8 · Crack the Whip

Cory sat alone. It seemed like forever.

Delphinius spun. He jumped. He landed on one leg. Then he took off around the rink. Backward. He wasn't wobbling now. Delphinius was a good skater. As good a skater as Cory. Maybe even better.

It wasn't fair. Cory wondered why his mother didn't see that it had all been Delphinius's fault. A trick. Just to get Cory in trouble.

Baltimore and Josh skated up. Baltimore's skates flashed, and chips of ice powder flew up as he stopped.

Josh stopped by grabbing the railing. He couldn't skate as well as Baltimore.

"Come on out on the ice," they said. "You're missing the party."

Then Cory's mother skated up. "Sorry, guys," she

said. "Cory needs some thinking time." She nudged them back onto the ice and skated away.

Cory's upper lip quivered. He felt like crying, but he wouldn't. He stuck out his tongue instead.

"Hey, Curly! Got a problem?" Delphinius glided by and didn't stop.

"You got a problem!" Cory mumbled.

Finally Cory's time was up. His mother skated up to him. "Have you sorted this out?" she asked.

Cory nodded. He had used his thinking time to sort out everything. He was tired of being pushed around by Delphinius. Sometimes you just had to stand up for yourself, and this was one of those times.

"Then you can come back onto the ice," said Cory's mother.

Cory's blades flashed as he hit the ice. He raced round and round the rink, zipping in and out. He passed Baltimore and Josh. "Meet me at the benches in five minutes," he said.

Then he glided past Tim. "Meet me at the benches."

Delphinius Lane had a problem all right. It was called Cory Coleman.

Five minutes later Cory glanced around the rink.

His mother and Ms. Ricks were at the snack counter. Delphinius was showing off in the middle of the rink.

"I'll show him," Cory said to himself. Then he explained his plan to Baltimore, Josh, and Tim.

"What if he gets hurt?" asked Tim.

"All we're going to do is scare him," said Cory. "No one's going to get hurt. Just make sure Delphinius is at the end of the whip."

"I don't know," said Baltimore. "He already gave me a bloody nose once."

"Delphinius isn't so bad." It was Josh. "All you have to do is stay out of his way. I don't know if this is such a great idea."

Cory was crushed. "Never mind, then!" he snapped. "I'll do it myself."

Cory blasted onto the ice. Round and round he skated.

Baltimore joined him first. He grabbed Cory's wrist and held tight. "You need people to crack the whip," he said.

On the next trip around the rink, Josh took hold of Baltimore's wrist. Tim hooked onto Josh's wrist.

Before long, the line grew into a slithering snake.

Each time it whipped around and across the rink, it grew longer and longer.

"Now!" Cory hollered. He fell out of line.

Baltimore took the lead. Then, as the end of the line came around, Cory hooked up again.

One by one by one, the whip snaked past Delphinius. "Come on, Delphinius," Cory hollered.

Delphinius glided to a stop.

The whip circled the rink one more time. Then it snaked past Delphinius again.

"Afraid?" Cory challenged.

Delphinius's freckles squished together as he smashed his lips together. He held out his arm. Cory grabbed it.

The whip snaked in and out. In and out. Faster and faster. Faster and faster, until the end was a blur.

"Crack!" Baltimore hollered.

The whip broke apart.

Cory jerked hard and let go of Delphinius's arm.

Delphinius sailed off toward the railing.

Whoosh! There was a loud, rushing, wheezing sound, like air from a blacksmith's bellows. Then Delphinius dropped to the ice.

9 · Liar

Delphinius lay on the ice. His knees were drawn up. His chest pushed up and down as he gasped for breath.

Up and down. Up and down.

Baltimore and Josh stared at Cory. They both spoke at once. "You said—"

But Cory heard his own words. *No one's going to get hurt.* And he felt a sick feeling deep in his stomach.

They raced toward Delphinius. Everyone else did too.

Then Cory's mother and Ms. Ricks were there. Ms. Ricks kneeled down on the ice and lifted Delphinius's head onto her lap.

Delphinius gulped for air.

"Take it easy," Ms. Ricks said calmly. "Take it easy. Breathe." She stroked his hair as she spoke. "That's right. Nice and deep."

"What happened?" It was Cory's mother.

No one answered.

Cory stared at the ice and gnawed on his tender thumb. He was afraid that if he looked at his mother, she'd know what had happened. She'd know that cracking the whip had been his idea. And she *would* know. Mothers *always* know.

Turning seven wasn't so great after all. Nothing had gone right. Not trying out his present. Not the party. Not scaring Delphinius. Cracking the whip was just supposed to teach Delphinius a lesson. It wasn't supposed to—

Cory shivered. Not because he was cold. What if something bad had happened to Delphinius? Something real bad. Cory didn't want to think about it. When he did, the sick feeling in his stomach came back. Only now, it was worse than sick.

Cory shook his head. He thought it might shake the nightmare thoughts away.

"It looks like you've had the breath knocked out

of you," Ms. Ricks told Delphinius. Then she looked up at Cory's mother. "He'll be all right. Something like this happens almost every week at school. He probably got a little careless."

Cory hoped it was true—that Delphinius would be all right. Ms. Ricks had just said so.

Just then, Delphinius pulled in a deep breath of air. "Unh-huh," he gasped. Tears began to tumble down his face. He sobbed and wiped his nose on his arm. Between sobs he said, "They— they're— always mean— to me. All of— them." That surprised Cory. He thought it was the other way around.

It must have been a surprise to C.J., too. She pushed her glasses up on her nose. "You started it," she said. "You were the one who went smashing into people first."

"That was— just— to get even— with him," Delphinius sobbed. He pointed at Cory. "I thought— if— I ruined his— party—" His voice trailed off.

Cory couldn't believe his ears. "What did I ever do to you?" he asked.

"Humpf!" Delphinius said. "Ever since the first day of school, you've been teasing me."

Cory's mouth became an O. His eyes got big. "Unh-huh. I never."

"He made fun of me because I wasn't upstairs in third grade like I was supposed to be," Delphinius said. He looked right at Baltimore when he said it.

Then Delphinius looked back at Cory. "And you called me Dumb-phinius."

Cory's mouth became a bigger O and his eyes got bigger. "I nev—"

"Liar!" Delphinius yelled. "I heard you." Then he began to sob again. "You— you think I didn't?"

Except for Delphinius's muffled sobs, it was quiet then.

Cory kicked at the ice with the toe of his blade. His sick feeling came back. Only this time, it was different.

Liar. It was true. Cory knew it was true.

He felt everyone's eyes on him. "I— I'm sorry," Cory said softly.

"I— I'm not *dumb*," Delphinius said between sobs.

"I— I just don't read so hot. Isn't that— isn't that right, Ms. Ricks?"

Ms. Ricks nodded her head. "Don't worry, Delphinius. You'll learn to read. I promise." Ms. Ricks's voice was soft and reassuring. She continued to stroke his hair.

Delphinius didn't look so tough anymore. To Cory's surprise, he wished there was something he could do to make things better. Just then he had an idea.

"Ms. Ricks, why don't we have reading buddies?" Cory said. "Like arithmetic buddies. Only for reading."

Ms. Ricks looked thoughtful for a minute. Then she said, "It just might work."

"Maybe I could be Delphinius's reading buddy," Cory suggested.

Ms. Ricks nodded. "It just might work," she said again. "If you'll be his reading buddy, maybe he'll be your arithmetic buddy. Delphinius is good at arithmetic. He's already halfway through the third-grade book."

"Wow!" everyone said.

"Delphinius, what do you think about that idea?" asked Ms. Ricks.

Delphinius looked up. His eyes were puffy and red. But his breathing was back to normal now, and his tears were gone. He sat up and rubbed his eyes.

"I— I guess," Delphinius said.

10 · A Surprise for Cory

Eleven o'clock. Everyone sang "Happy Birthday." But it had not been a happy birthday. Cory was not happy at all.

Outside the skating rink, Elizabeth Ann's mother's car was parked in a cloud of gray smoke. Elizabeth Ann and Tim waved good-bye to Cory. Then the car sputtered through the parking lot. Cory noticed that they both ducked down when Mr. Lewis turned into the parking lot in his shiny, black car.

C.J. wished Cory a happy birthday. Then she climbed into the black Mercedes.

Amy and Josh raced away together, Josh on the bicycle, Amy on foot.

"We'll drop you," Cory's mother said to Delphinius. Everyone else was gone now. Even Ms. Ricks.

It was a silent drive to Delphinius's house. Cory wished someone would say something. But no one did.

Finally, Cory's mother wheeled the Subaru into Delphinius's driveway. Delphinius hopped out of the front seat. "Thanks for the ride," he said.

"D— Delphinius." Cory stumbled over the word. He didn't know what to say. But he wanted to say something. "I— I'm sorry about— what happened. And everything."

Delphinius shrugged and headed up to the door.

"Hey, Del," Cory yelled. *Del.* It just blurted out all of a sudden—like they were old friends or something. "Forgot your skates." Cory jumped out of the backseat. He darted up to the door and offered them to Delphinius.

"Thanks," Delphinius said. Then he pushed open the door. "And happy birthday."

They were on their way home then. Cory's mind was a jumble of thoughts. He wanted to tell his mother everything. About Delphinius. About the Monster Wheels. About how rotten he felt. But when he opened his mouth, no words came out.

The car swung into the driveway. Baltimore and

"People make mistakes. Even grown-ups," Cory's mother said. This time her voice was soft. "I'm sorry I blamed you when Delphinius skated into Ms. Ricks and me." Cory gave his mother a great big hug.

After a while his mother said, "I still think you should open your presents."

Cory didn't understand. But he was too exhausted to explain everything again.

He reached for the present from his mother. The Monster Wheels. He unwrapped it and took it out of the box.

"Try it out," Cory's mother said.

"But—"

Cory's mother put her finger to her lips. "Shhh," she said. "Just try it out."

Cory put the Monster Wheels on the floor. He aimed the remote control at the hot-red truck and pushed the lever.

Va-roooom! The Monster Wheels took off across the floor. Cory jerked the lever back to stop it.

"You— you knew," Cory accused.

His mother smiled and nodded.

"But how?"

"It wasn't hard to figure out," Cory's mother said. "You forgot to put the batteries back in the flashlight." She laughed softly. "I left that out to remind me to put batteries on the shopping list. The ones in the flashlight were dead, and I needed some extra for your Monster Wheels."

"Dead?" Cory asked. "You mean all that worry was—"

Cory didn't finish. He was laughing too hard to say another word. His mother laughed too.

On Monday, Cory went to school. Ms. Ricks had all the desks in twos.

A "Reading Buddies" map hung on the wall. It was a map of the room. There were fifteen squares on the map. One for each person in Ms. Ricks's room, including Ms. Ricks.

Cory found his name on the map. DELPHINIUS was printed in the next square.

"Find your seats for reading," Ms. Ricks said. Chairs clattered. Voices buzzed. Feet shuffled.

Delphinius raised his hand. "Can I be book monitor again?" he asked. "I mean . . . 'May I?' "

"May I help too?" It was Cory. He was eager to get started.

"Two book monitors would be nice," Ms. Ricks said. "Thank you."

Then the roomed buzzed with noise as each person read quietly to a partner.

Delphinius read, " 'The wa— wa—' "

Cory covered the back part of the word. "What does that say?" he asked. "Dogs do it with their tails."

"Wag," said Delphinius.

"Now," said Cory. "What's this?" He covered the *w a g.*

"That's easy," Delphinius said. " 'On.' Wag. On." He snapped his fingers. " 'Wagon.' "

"Right," Cory said.

Delphinius smiled. His freckles seemed to multiply when he did. And Cory thought, Freckles are nice.

Then Delphinius began to read again. " 'The wagon rolled down the hill.' "

Suddenly Delphinius stopped. " 'Fas— ter,' " he stammered.

"Faster," Cory said.

"Oh. Right." Delphinius read, " 'Faster and faster it rolled. Faster and faster.' "

Cory felt good. Maybe the Delphinius problem was over. Delphinius was reading. It wasn't perfect reading. Not yet. But it was only the first day of reading buddies.